The King of the Hummingbirds and Other Tales

JOHN GARDNER

THE KING OF THE HUMMINGBIRDS
and Other Tales

Illustrated by Michael Sporn

ALFRED A. KNOPF · NEW YORK

THIS IS A BORZOI BOOK PUBLISHED BY ALFRED A. KNOPF, INC.

Text Copyright © 1977 by Boskydell Artists Ltd. Illustrations Copyright © 1977 by Michael Sporn. All rights reserved under International and Pan-American Copyright Conventions. Published in the United States by Alfred A. Knopf, Inc., New York, and simultaneously in Canada by Random House of Canada Limited, Toronto. Distributed by Random House, Inc., New York. Library of Congress Cataloging in Publication Data
Gardner, John Champlin, 1933—   The king of the hummingbirds, and other tales. SUM-MARY: *Four fairy tales featuring a stupid coppersmith's son, a witch unhappy in her profession, a gnome with power to change things, and a fat, bespectacled Jewish boy who hopes to marry a princess. 1. Fairy tales. [1. Fairy tales] I. Sporn, Michael. II. Title. PZ8.G216Ki [Fic] 76-42457 ISBN 0-394-83319-8 ISBN 0-394-93319-2 lib. bdg. Manufactured in the United States of America 098765432*

To Francesca and wee Fred

CONTENTS

The King of the Hummingbirds

There was once a young man who was stupider than most but had one great virtue: he could always see everything from the other person's side. The result was that he had a great many friends, and wherever he went there was usually peace and quiet, at least for a while.

One day the young man was walking in the woods, and he came upon a hummingbird lying on its back, kicking its legs and peeping as if fit to be tied.

"Perhaps it has hurt its wing," the young man thought. "If I had a broken wing, I would want some kind stranger to pick me up and make me a splint." But he didn't know how to make a splint, so he decided that perhaps the hummingbird was grieving because it had been disappointed in love. "In that case," the young man thought, "I would want some kind friend to intercede for me with my beloved." But while the young man was thinking this, a tiny voice said, "Young man, come here." It was the hummingbird.

The young man did as he was told and knelt beside the bird. As soon as he was near he saw the truth. The bird was dying of some dread disease, or else old age, or perhaps from being shot.

"Young man," said the bird, speaking with great difficulty, "I see you have a kindly face. I have no one else to turn to, so I must put my faith in you."

"You can trust me," the young man said. "I'm not clever, but it's true that I'm kindly."

"It will have to do," the hummingbird said. It coughed and closed its eyes for a moment, then spoke again—hoarsely, for a bird. "I am the king of the hummingbirds, and all my kingdom depends on me, but unfortunately I am dying without an heir. Since you are the only one at hand, I must ask you to take my place. Rule justly, my son. Never let the power go to your head. Take the ring from my foot. It will identify you to my flock." Without another word, the king of the hummingbirds jerked twice and lay dead as a doornail.

The young man was astonished and grieved, though they were strangers, and he did all he knew how (which wasn't much) to revive the poor hummingbird, but to no avail. So he took the ring the bird had mentioned and hung it on a string around his neck, and then he dug a small grave and buried the bird and put a stone where its feet were. After that, the new king of the hummingbirds went home.

Now this young man, whose name was Olaf, was the lastborn son of a somewhat self-centered coppersmith who had hopes of rising in the world and becoming a

4

knight. Olaf's two brothers were clever and gallant, so the coppersmith had sent them away to school, hoping they might learn the ins and outs of things and help him. Poor young Olaf, being hopelessly stupid and much too kindly to make even a good fisherman, was left at home to patch old kettles and copper lamps.

As soon as he stepped in the door, his father said, "Olaf, where have you been? There's kettles piled to the ceiling, and you out dawdling."

Olaf hung his head and said, "Sorry, sir," and hurried to the shop to work.

His mother, who loved him dearly—partly because she was a little slow herself, though she was pretty as a queen (yet somehow her husband didn't love her as he ought)—brought Olaf a pickle and some milk.

"Poor Olaf," she said, patting his shoulder. "Poor, good Olaf! What's the meaning of it all!"

"Well," said Olaf, "it's not as bad as it might be. I may be more important than some people think."

His mother smiled sadly, patting him again, wondering if her son might be crazy. Then she went to bed.

Olaf worked all night, as usual, but at least he was not lonely. The ants on whom he had refrained from stepping came and paraded by while he worked; the mice he'd fed cheese came and polished the copper pots by rubbing their backs against them; the owls he'd allowed to roost on the rafters flew down to him and fanned Olaf's fire with their wings; the wolves he'd allowed to hide under his bench when there were hunters about came and helped him to line up the pots when he'd finished with the mending; and the huge, burly thieves he'd allowed into the cellar when they escaped from the sheriff (who'd gotten trapped in conversation with the mayor) sang him barbershop quartets. So the work went quickly, and when he was through Olaf stretched out by the fire and wondered what he could do, now that he was king, for his people. "I wonder if I should assemble my parliament," he mused. However, since he wasn't certain what a parliament was, he let it go and fell sound asleep. Immediately the mice began chasing the ants, and the owls began chasing the mice, the wolves began chasing the owls, and the huge, burly thieves began hitting at the wolves with their big heavy clubs. Such was the world whenever Olaf turned his back. Soon the room was completely empty, except for Olaf, and the fire had shriveled to an ash.

Now as luck would have it, the king of the kingdom where Olaf lived had one great passion, and that was walking in the garden with his daughter the princess. Everything was all right until one day when, as he closed the garden gate, the thorn of a rose got caught in the lock in just such a way that not even wizardry

could open it. As the thorn got stiffer and stiffer, for lack of moisture, the lock got more and more difficult to open. And the more days that passed with the gate unopened, the more the blowing sand sealed up the crack. The more the sand sealed up the crack, the darker that part of the wall became, and the more the honeybees who lived in the garden began to build their hives there. That wouldn't have been so bad, but the more the honeybees built hives on that wall, the more the bears from the surrounding woods began to climb over the wall for the honey. The king tried everything, but nothing worked. The wall was too high for a man to climb and also too covered with honeybees; the gate wouldn't budge, and any excessive commotion would stir up the bears into a dangerous wrath. It was bad enough that the king could no longer walk in his garden, but that was not the worst of it. He had inadvertently closed the gate before the princess was out. She was therefore still in there, and she was deathly afraid of bears.

The king sent out a proclamation that whoever could open the garden gate would have half the kingdom and his daughter's hand in marriage.

Everyone came from miles around, from knights to cobblers, but no one had any luck. At last the coppersmith sent his two eldest sons. This, he thought, would be his big chance. If one of his sons became a king, he himself would become, surely, at least a knight. Olaf, however, he refused to allow to go. Olaf hung his head, understanding exactly how his father felt. But he muttered to his mother in privacy, "Just the same, I may be more important than some people think." His mother smiled sadly and patted him on the shoulder and felt depressed.

"Your Majesty," said the eldest son of the coppersmith when he got to the castle, "I've come to unlock that gate."

"Talk's cheap," said the king. He waved the young man off in the general direction of the garden, and he did not even bother to go with him. He'd seen many a failure these past few weeks, and he was losing interest.

Now the coppersmith's eldest son had one great virtue, which was that he always saw through to the heart of a problem. And so he did in this case. He packed dynamite all around the gate and unwound the fuse till he could place the plunger in the middle of the castle yard, a hundred feet away. Then he called out, "Stand back, princess." But at the sound of his voice, a huge bear came over the wall and began to chase him, just as he'd chased off a hundred before him. And so the eldest son failed and was humiliated and left his equipment there and never again dared show his face in public. Then it was the second eldest's turn.

The second eldest had a different virtue. He always did everything in style, for, as he sometimes explained, "People don't remember a man so much for *what* he does. They remember him for the flourish with which he does it." (Which is true.) So the first thing the second eldest did was tie his majestic white horse to a tree, and the second thing he did was cover the garden gate with orchids. Then, calling, "Stand back, princess!" he picked up a huge golden battering ram and began to hurl himself at the gate. But halfway there he changed his mind, for the orchids had attracted the attention of the bears and two of them were coming straight at him, and it wasn't worth the candle. So the second son failed as the first had failed, and he left his equipment and dropped out of public view.

"Ruined!" said the coppersmith.

"There's still Olaf," said his wife.

The coppersmith scoffed, having no respect for his wife's opinions; but then, on second thought, he told Olaf to go over to the castle and work on that gate.

"Yes sir," Olaf said, understanding how his mother and father felt and seeing that whichever way he turned his case was hopeless. Nevertheless he combed his hair, and his mother packed him a lunch, and, followed by his ants, mice, owls, and wolves, he set out. Part way to the castle he met the band of huge, burly thieves he'd done a favor once, and since he had no plan worked out yet and knew that sometimes a man could use helpers, he asked if they'd go to the castle with him, and for old times' sake they said yes.

When they'd gone a little ways, they met the king's sheriff, who'd been after that band of huge, burly thieves for years, and Olaf asked timidly, "Could I borrow your horse, sheriff?" For the sheriff was his friend, and he didn't want to be tired and sweaty when he broke down the garden gate and rescued the princess, in case he should.

"Well, all right," said the sheriff, because Olaf was his friend and because it would be handy, he thought, to know exactly where those thieves were. The sheriff got down and walked with the thieves, and Olaf rode ahead on the palomino.

They went a little farther and they met the village mayor, who had been trying for years to get in good with the sheriff for political reasons. When Olaf saw the mayor in all his finery, he said, "Excuse me, mayor. Could I possibly borrow your coat and hat so I don't look like a common peasant when I rescue the princess, in case I do?"

"Well," the mayor said, liking young Olaf and thinking an act of kindness might impress the sheriff, "all right, if you really need them." So Olaf put them on, and the village mayor came walking along behind him with the sheriff and the others until they came to the front of the castle, where the king was playing quoits.

"Sir," said Olaf apologetically, understanding exactly how the king must feel, interrupted at his game, "my friends and I have come to try to rescue the princess."

The king put on his glasses and stood dangling his quoits. "And who the devil are *you?*" he said.

Olaf said, "I'm Olaf, king of the hummingbirds."

"Hah!" said the king. He tapped his chin. Then, tossing his quoits away and signaling to his knights and servants, as well as to the coppersmith and Olaf's mother, who'd decided to come watch, the king said grimly, "*This* I have got to see." And they all went to the gate that wouldn't open.

The situation was more hopeless than ever, and everyone knew it, even (in a dim way) the coppersmith's son Olaf. The thorn inside the lock was as dry as a bone, so that nothing in this world could budge it. The sand which sealed up the crack between the gate and the gatepost was as solid as cement, and all over the gate there were honeybees and goo, and the garden was now so full of bears that the princess would have been dead for sure had the bears not luckily preferred honey.

"What's your plan?" the king whispered. Everyone was speaking in whispers now, since no one wanted to disturb the ferocious bears.

"You'll see," whispered the king of the hummingbirds hopefully. The truth was, he hadn't yet thought of a plan. Indeed, he only very vaguely understood what the problem was. To stall for time, he had the thieves step back and took off the village mayor's coat and hat and rolled up his shirtsleeves. Still nothing came to him, and to stall for more time, he slowly removed his shirt.

"Very strange," the village mayor whispered ingratiatingly to the sheriff.

"Very strange," said the sheriff in a friendly voice to the thieves.

And strange indeed it was. For hovering over the orchids left by the second-eldest son there was a hummingbird, and beside the wall six feet away there was another. No sooner had Olaf, king of the hummingbirds, removed his shirt than both his subjects, in the same flash of sunlight, perceived the ring on the string around his neck and recognized their lord. They whistled, and in half a second there were hundreds upon thousands of hummingbirds, all whistling and humming their wings for pure delight. The roar of their wings was like a huge droning storm so fierce that the bees all came hurrying from their dark damp hives in alarm, and the bears inside grew so befuddled they couldn't climb the wall. As the bees came swarming out to see what was happening, the thieves and the sheriff and the village mayor and all the king's lords

and knights and servants, not to mention the wolves, owls, mice, and ants, began running about crazily this way and that, dancing and swatting at the bees in a perfect frenzy. The wind from the wings of the birds and bees and the running, swatting friends of Olaf shook the sand from the gate and let the honey drip down on the stiff little thorn, and it softened and bent, and the lock suddenly snapped open. At once the bears came charging out, but just then Olaf's second-eldest brother's majestic white horse broke loose from his tree, upset by the commotion, and he tripped on the golden ramrod and fell with all his might on Olaf's eldest brother's dynamite plunger, and the bears and orchids and a few of the bees were blown so high that some of the petals and fur are even now still coming down again.

"Wow!" cried the princess, looking around herself, wide-eyed. Then she said, as if knowing exactly what Olaf had been thinking, "What *will* we do with all these hummingbirds?"

"We will rule them justly," said Olaf. "Or perhaps get someone else to rule them. Or possibly turn them loose."

"Why don't *I* be king of the hummingbirds," Olaf's father said, since a king was obviously better than a knight, and he was insatiably ambitious.

"Sure, fine," said Olaf.

And now Olaf suddenly discovered he was alone with the princess. His father had run off noisily shouting, chasing his hummingbirds, trying to organize a parliament. The sheriff, with the mayor running close behind, had left to chase the thieves, and the thieves, along with some of the ants, were in the garden stealing honey. The king, who happened to be a widower, had gone for a walk with Olaf's mother, followed by most of the wolves, owls, and mice, and Olaf's two brothers who had failed hadn't come in the first place.

"King of the hummingbirds," the princess was saying, tapping her pretty, dimpled chin and smiling, possibly making fun of Olaf. "Crazy!"

"I'm not sure I understand you," said Olaf, somewhat uncomfortably.

"Never mind, birdbrain," said the princess and gave him a little pat. "Let's start cleaning up this mess."

The Witch's Wish

In a certain kingdom there lived a wicked, disgusting old witch whose greatest pleasure in life was burning down synagogues and churches. In the beginning she set fire to them at the stroke of midnight, when no one was about; but later she grew more brazen and would often be seen lurking nearby, hiding behind a tree or peeking around past one of the parked cars in the parking lot, when the congregation was just leaving at the end of the service. One evening, feeling more brazen than usual, the wicked old witch slunk into a church or, possibly, synagogue while the service was still going. Since she didn't want to burn down the church with people still inside it—such a thing would never have crossed her mind, for witch or no witch, she had about her a certain innate tenderheartedness— she seated herself inconspicuously in a pew at the back and waited for the service to be over. Without giving much thought to what she was doing, she began to listen to the sermon; and lo and behold, before she knew what was happening, she was converted.

The old witch's hands began to shake, and tears ran down her leathery old cheeks. "I have sinned unspeakably," she moaned. "What can I ever do to make it up?"

The congregation got to its feet to sing a final hymn, but the wicked old witch paid no attention, for she was lost in thought.

"First off," she mused, "I must stop being a witch." But one question among many was, if she stopped being a witch, then just what *would* she be? She wrung her hands and bit her lips together—and then she got an idea: "I can sell paper flowers in the city," she thought, "and give all my money to the poor."

She almost laughed aloud, she was so delighted. And oddly enough, her delight at the thought of her new life so changed her features that strangers going past her pew (for the congregation was now leaving) thought to themselves, "What a sweet little old lady! Who can she be?"

When the old witch realized that the service was over, she got up and left the church. As fast as her legs would carry her, she went to find the queen of the witches, who lived in a hollow tree in the center of the forest. The queen of the witches was so cruel and ugly that at sight of her face an ordinary person would fall dead on the spot. All but the bravest of the witches closed their eyes whenever the queen came in sight, and as a matter of fact when she looked in the mirror, even the queen herself felt a little bit woozy.

The witch knocked on the queen's door and called out timidly, "Yoo-hoo!"

The door opened about ten inches, and there stood

the horrible, horrible queen of the witches.

The old witch reeled at the sight, but, bracing herself, she looked the queen in the eye. "I've come to ask if you would mind if I stopped being a witch," she asked. "Tonight I went to burn down a church and, I'm sorry to say, I was converted."

"Zam booey!" exclaimed the queen, throwing the door wide open. "Come on in and tell me all about it!"

"There's nothing to tell, really," said the witch, entering the queen's modestly furnished apartment. "I just want to stop being a witch."

The queen took the witch's hand and led her to a chair near the fireplace where a huge cauldron was steaming and bubbling. When the witch's knock came, the queen had been preparing a brew that would turn people's pet parakeets into bats.

"What kind of church was it?" asked the queen, lowering her grizzly eyebrows. "Was it a Presbyterian church? A Baptist church? A Jewish Orthodox synagogue? Was it Lutheran? Episcopalian? Buddhist? Islamic?"

"I didn't notice," said the witch, glancing about her in confusion.

"You didn't notice!" the queen of the witches exclaimed. She bit her lips and squinted, calming herself. Gently she prodded, "Was it a Christ Brethren church, perhaps?" She leaned closer. "Was it a Russian Greek Friends' church? A Hungarian Emmanuel Baptist church? Was it the African Methodist church?"

"I don't know! I didn't pay attention!" cried the witch. "I had no idea it was important."

"It makes all the difference in the world," the queen said soberly, her eyes mere slits. She studied a spider's web she'd been working on all day, for in the daytime the queen of the witches was a spider. "I've been converted sixty-seven times, myself," said the queen. "I must say, it never made me want to stop being a witch. In fact, rather the opposite. I suppose it hits some people differently from the way it hits others." Then she drew up a great plush chair which had a canopy over it like a four-poster bed and heavy side curtains of wine-black velvet, and sat down beside her visitor. "Well, well, well," she said, "so you want to stop being a witch!" She frowned, weighing the matter. Then she shook her head and reached out absently to stir the brew in the cauldron. Small, grotesque creatures of a kind not normally seen in the world were jumping around in it, happy as lizards, for broiling heat was their element. "Really, you know, it's impossible," said the queen of the witches. "If I *did* know a way out, how could I in good conscience tell you? Think of the confusion if Satanists should turn ecumenical!"

They sat in silence for a time, gazing without interest at the two skeletons seated on the chesterfield reading through the evening news.

Then the witch said tentatively, "I did wish I might sell paper flowers and give my money to the poor."

"It would be a pleasant life, all right," said the queen with a sigh. "I've thought of it myself. Still, you must look at it this way: we witches have our pleasures too. Can sweet old ladies put hexes on television aerials so that people's pictures come in sideways? Can sweet old ladies put tree toads in candy machines so that the kid puts in his fifteen cents and—*Yipes!!?* Or put cats in front of blind men's seeing-eye dogs, heh heh? Or put wads of gum on the bottoms of bankers' canes?"

"All that's very pleasant, I'll admit," said the witch, and couldn't help but smile, "but it's nothing compared to stretching out a helping hand to the sick and needy, or giving money to the poor."

"Perhaps not," said the queen of witches irritably, for her visitor had her and she knew it, "but you can't have everything. Anyway, you can't stop being a witch just because you want to. It's against the rules, like trying to stop being a Mormon."

"I was afraid you'd say that," said the witch. "I suppose I'll just have to go on burning down synagogues and churches. But my heart won't be in it." So saying, she got up to leave.

"My dear," said the queen as the witch was about to go, "if I were you I'd take the shortcut home." She smiled slyly and gave her friend a wink.

"Whatever you think best," said the witch, rather puzzled, and she left.

As the witch was walking home through the forest, taking the shortcut as the queen had suggested, she came to a great, dark pool. The water in the pool lay perfectly still, covered over with dark green like a great, slimy carpet, and you would have thought nothing had stirred the surface of that pool for a hundred years. All around the pool there were gnarled old roots and dreadful looking flowers that mysteriously glowed in the dark like deep-toned jewels.

Looking into the pool, the witch said to herself morosely, "I wish—"

"Watch out!" cried a voice.

"I beg your pardon?" the witch exclaimed with a jump, for the voice had startled her half out of her wits. She looked all around, but she couldn't make out who had spoken to her.

"I said 'Watch out,'" said the voice. It was a large old toad with a tiny, elegant silver crown, sitting on a root at the opposite side of the pool. The toad continued, speaking very slowly—for the truth is he was stupid—"You have to be careful what you wish around here. This is a wishing pool. See all those tombstones over there?"

The witch looked, and there among the trees, sure enough, were a number of tombstones.

X "Those are the graves of people who happened to stand near the pool and say, QUOTE, I wish I were dead, END QUOTE."

"Why do you shout so?" asked the witch, her hands over her ears.

"I only shouted QUOTE and END QUOTE," said the toad. "I didn't want the pool to think I was making the wish myself. A person can't be too careful."

"I see," said the witch. Then she said, "Excuse my curiosity, but do you ever make any wishes of your own?"

"Only once," said the toad, rolling his eyes heavenward. "I used to be a handsome prince, but I hated it. I was lousy at it, to tell you the truth. One day as I was walking past the wishing pool, I said to myself, 'I wish I were a toad,' and *zam,* it happened."

"*Zam booey* you mean," the witch said.

"Yes, zam booey," the toad corrected himself, looking terribly embarrassed. "That's the expression." He sighed. "I always get it wrong."

"Don't you like being a toad?" the witch asked, for they were straying, she felt, from the subject.

"It's awful, I assure you. You should see the things toads eat!"

"How unpleasant for you," said the witch. "But if you don't like being a toad, why don't you wish yourself back into a handsome prince?"

"Well," said the toad, scratching his ear thought-

26

fully, "I didn't like being a prince either, you see. I was always falling off my horse, or knocking my crown off by not bending low enough when I walked through doors. Every time I ran I'd trip over my sword, and when the royal fool told jokes, I could never get them."

The witch sighed sympathetically. "It's a sad predicament," she said.

"Yes, it is," said the toad with a look of surprise. He hadn't thought of it before. "But tell me, what were *you* about to wish?"

"Well, I was about to wish—"

"SHE WAS ABOUT TO WISH BUT SHE DOESN'T WISH NOW!" the toad broke in loudly, making sure it was clear to the pool, which was even stupider than he was.

"Yes, I was *about* to wish that I had never been born."

"Oh my! How distressing! That's the worst of all possible things to wish!" cried the toad, breaking into a sweat. "What on earth can have driven you to that?"

The witch told him the whole story, and the toad listened politely and attentively, head cocked. When the story was over the toad said, "Why it's perfectly simple: all you have to do is wish you were a sweet old lady selling flowers and giving all her money to the poor." Then the toad fell into a brown study. "However," he said at last, lifting one long, webbed finger, "you must be sure it's what you really want. There's something to be said, of course, for being a sweet old

lady; but on the other hand, surely there's something to be said for your present occupation. What is the life of a witch like, exactly?"

"We occasionally burn down synagogues and churches," the witch said.

"Hmm," said the toad and winced, barely hiding his disgust.

"And we mix up babies in their cradles, so they grow up in the wrong families, and the rich ones feel foolishly good about themselves, and the poor ones that were supposed to be rich grow up feeling inferior."

"Hmm," said the toad once again, this time smiling to himself.

"And we change the signs on city busses and trains so that people get on and ride and ride for hours. And we put salt in people's sugar bowls and sugar in people's salt cellars. And we buy things on people's credit cards, and drop pencils down into people's pianos, and make holes in people's change pockets and—"

"Really?" said the toad excitedly. "Really? *Really*? What else?"

"Well, let me see," said the witch. "Sometimes we put sand in people's gas tanks. And sometimes, on Halloween, we put cherry bombs in people's fireplaces."

"Good heavens!" cried the toad. "Isn't that rather likely to damage the flue?"

"We only do it on Halloween," said the witch. "But you can see why I want to get into some other line."

"Hmm," said the toad, looking up at the sky and smiling from ear to ear, scratching his elbow. "Hmmmmm."

"Yes, I've definitely decided," said the witch, and she stepped to the edge of the wishing pool. "I wish," she said, shutting her eyes and folding her hands tightly, "I wish I were a sweet old lady selling flowers in the city and giving away my money to the poor!"

That very instant the witch vanished. She reappeared standing on a corner in the city selling yellow paper flowers and giving away all her money to the poor. Snow fell dismally all around her and the cold made her fingers blue; she shivered and coughed and hugged herself in her shawl and she cried out, "Paper flowers" in a feeble little voice. Nevertheless, she was serenely happy, for doing good nearly always makes people happy.

Meanwhile, back at the wishing pool, the toad sat looking up at the sky thoughtfully and scratching his chin. He scratched and thought, and thought and scratched, for a long, long time. At last, in a loud, clear voice he said to the pool, "I WISH I WERE A WITCH!"

Instantly, with a great, glorious smile, the toad vanished. And ever after that day, the toad was the happiest witch in all the kingdom.

The Pear Tree

The most beautiful pear tree in the world," said the king of the elves.

"The most beautiful, yes," said the queen. Her eyes shone.

"Ah!" said all the elves.

Then they turned it into a dewdrop and hid it in a rose and laughed with glee, and they sat down to watch.

Along came a knight all in armor of yellow gold, and drew up his horse where he knew by experience the pear tree stood, and tied up his horse and got down. He looked where he knew the pear tree was, but the pear tree was gone. He scowled and tipped up his helmet and reconsidered and looked to the left, but still it was not there, nor was it to the right. It was nowhere. "Ruined," said the knight, looking up toward heaven. Then he noticed the rose and went over to it and said to himself, "Since I can't take the princess the perfect pear, maybe I should take her this rose, and maybe she'll be so touched she'll ask her father the king of the people to stop and reconsider."

He reached out toward the rose, his forehead thoughtful, and the elves waited tensely, for it seemed unnatural that a knight should pass their test; but then, sure enough, the knight drew back his hand. "Ha," he said. "She'd laugh in my face." He went back to his horse and rode away, and the elves laughed till their faces were wet with tears.

"Hush!" said the king of the elves.

"Hush!" said the queen.

Along came a rich merchant, riding in a carriage of yellow gold, and he stopped where he knew the pear tree was. He pointed, and two of his servants got out to look for the pear tree, but it was nowhere.

The merchant scowled, banged the dottle from his pipe, then got down, huffing and puffing, to see for himself. But still no pear tree. "Blast," said the merchant. One of the servants said, "Shall I cut you a rose, sir?" He stood prepared to cut off the rose with some scissors.

The merchant waved it away in disgust. "Let's go home."

Again the elves laughed merrily, but only for a moment. For hardly was the merchant out of sight when who should come along but a well-known poet with a solid gold walking stick. The poet saw that the pear tree was gone, which was more or less what he'd expected, and noticed the rose and went over to stand by it, hands on hips. He shook his head sadly and extemporized, making as original a poem as he knew how:

O Rose, thou art sick!
The invisible bug
That flies in the whirlwind
To give you a hug,
Has found out your bed
Of red, red light,
And his dark, secret love
Has given you blight.

He snapped the rose from the stem, considered it a moment, then dropped it to the ground. The elves all dashed out to put the dewdrop back in.

The poet looked up at the clouds and frowned, then thought about the rose. "I should take it back to the princess," he said to himself, "as a metaphor of the shortness of life and the certainty of failure." But on second thought he said, "She'd never get it." So he went his way.

The elves laughed nervously, not certain *they* got it either.

Then came Eddie.

Eddie was the only son of a poor Jewish blacksmith. He was a quiet, soft-spoken boy who was fat and wore spectacles and had read, in perfect innocence, many books. Every night before he went to bed he put out a saucer of milk for the elves, under the misapprehension (from something he'd read) that elves like milk.

The elves were touched by this, and they drank the milk, winter and summer, though milk made them gag. When the king of the people said, "My daughter is old enough to marry, so I will give her hand to whoever brings her a single perfect pear," Eddie's old father and mother said, "Eddie, why don't you see can you marry the princess? You're a good boy, you ought to be a prince."

He didn't believe he had a chance, but he said, "I'll give it a try." So now he had come to where the pear tree was, and he looked and saw, as the others had seen, no pear tree.

He put his fists on his hips.

Although he had never believed he had a chance, he was more disappointed than he'd imagined he would be, for the princess was beautiful and gentle and they liked the same things, and it's royal marriages like that that make kingdoms safe and happy. In fact he was so sad he had to take off his glasses and wipe them. The elves crossed their fingers and began to worry that the test was unreasonably hard.

But when Eddie had wiped his glasses, he noticed the rose, and immediately, without thinking, he picked it up and carried it away with him. And the elves danced with glee.

As luck would have it, it began to rain, and Eddie had to run, his stomach bouncing up and down and his

cheeks puffing out and in. Twice the dewdrop fell out
of the rose and the elves had to sort through the rain-
drops for it and sneak it back into the rose in Eddie's
hand. Then at last he was home.

"So where's the pear?" Eddie's mama said.

"The tree's disappeared," said Eddie, and sighed.

"Disappeared?" she said. "It was there this morning.
I saw it with these two eyes!"

Eddie shrugged. "Well, now it's gone, Mama." He
put out milk for the elves, with an umbrella to keep
the rain off, and he went up to his bed with a book.

Weeks passed. All he did with the rose was look at it
sometimes in the morning and sigh a little, thinking
how he'd missed out on marrying the nicest girl in all
the kingdom. The elves shook their heads.

"I'd have sworn he'd take it to the princess," said the
king of the elves.

"Well, you were wrong," said the queen. "You and
your ideas."

"Well, you went along with it," said the king. "You
didn't believe me you should have said no. You think
I'm God, maybe?"

"*Oy vay*," said the queen. "Always God. All he can
talk about is God. He should have been a rabbi."

For two weeks after that they didn't speak.

But the rose never withered, because of the magical
dewdrop, which was really the pear tree, the most

beautiful pear tree in the world. Eventually Eddie noticed this. "Funny rose," he said to himself, and interlaced his fingers. The next morning he looked again, and still no withering. He decided to give it to the princess, for no special reason. He was in love.

He said, "Hey, Papa, I have to run over to the castle."

"Castle, Eddie?" his papa said.

"Oh, I got this funny rose," Eddie said. "I thought I'd give it to the princess."

"That's a good boy," Eddie's papa said. "She'll like it."

So he went to the castle, and the elves all rode in his hair, as light as feathers.

The guards said, "You want something, man?"

"I'll tell you," Eddie said, removing his glasses. "I picked up this funny rose somewhere. What's interesting about it is, it never seems to wither. Funny?"

"Funny, sure," the guards said. "How we know you telling the truth?"

Eddie thought about it, then he shrugged. "So keep it awhile," he said. And he gave it to the guards at the gate and walked back home.

The queen of the elves said, "This kid's a loser. Why didn't we leave her have the knight with the yellow-gold clothes?"

"Pah," said the king of the elves, "better the merchant. Security. What do you think it would be like,

living with a knight. Always away on the road someplace. No, better a good, steady merchant.''

"Ech," said the queen. "He was too old. Better the
poet, except he was a string bean."

"Eddie's fat," the king said happily.

"That's true," said the queen, softening. "Make
somebody a good husband."

Two or three weeks later, Eddie went back to the
castle and said, "How'd it turn out, man?"

The guards looked at each other and shrugged.

"You know," Eddie said, "the rose."

Still they looked blank. "You sure it's one of us you
talked to, not the cat that works nights?"

Eddie laughed. "Hey come on, you guys, don't kid
around. You got my rose someplace?"

"Man, if there was a rose around here we'd see it,
you dig? Look how clean we keep it." They waved for
him to look around the gatehouse. But the elves slipped the rose from under the visitors' book up onto the
top of the table and Eddie saw it. It was smashed a
little from being under the book, but it still wasn't
withered.

"Oh, there it is," Eddie said. "Good as new, too.
Mind if I take it to the princess?"

"You kidding?" the guards said. "Tonight's her
wedding night."

Eddie looked horrified, his eyes as round as his
glasses, and so the guards took pity on him.

"Dude came along with this pear," the guards said. "It wasn't much, you ask me. But the king was bored with the whole thing, so he decided to allow it. It's a crying shame, you ask *me*, brother. This dude that got her, he looks like a bear in clothes."

"*Oy!*" Eddie said. He put his hands to the sides of his head. After a while he said, "Maybe I could slip the rose in under her door?" He had to wipe his glasses. The guards were sorry for him.

"We don't see you pass, we can't very well stop you, brother," they said. They looked up at the trees and started humming, jiving with the birds. Eddie stood there in a moral quandary. The elves got a running jump and gave him a shove, and in he went.

When he knocked on the princess's door, a funny thing happened. He'd just finished knocking, and the princess was just starting to open the door when, *zap*, a pear tree grew out of the rose.

"Wow," said Eddie, and lowered his eyebrows and looked at it.

"You knocked?" said the princess. Then she saw the pear tree, loaded with pears, the most beautiful pears in the world. "Say!" she said.

"I thought you'd like—" Eddie began.

"One sec," said the princess. She went back inside, where there was a man. "Rupert," she said, "I have the worst headache. Do you mind?"

He left. He looked like a bear in clothes.

The princess smiled and said, "Come on in, tall dark and handsome. Excuse me just a sec, while I slip into something more comfortable."

He pretended to salute, hand cupped; it was a gesture he had.

"Where do you want the pear tree?" Eddie asked.

The elves laughed with glee. They were so happy they turned the perfect pears into diamonds and rubies; but when the princess came back she was disappointed, so they turned them back to pears. Except for one, which remains a ruby to this day, and if you want to know more, put out some milk and ask for Irving.

The Gnome and
the Dragon

Once upon a time, in a strange country, there lived an incredibly ugly little gnome who was a great artist, changing the world around any way he pleased, whether from boredom or for nobler reasons. Reality was putty in the clever gnome's hands, as it would be in the hands of a whittler or a fiddler or a teller of moralizing tales. He could change anything to anything and could even change him*self* to anything, or even into twenty things at once. He changed reality so frequently by his magic that in the end he lost track of it, for all he ever thought was "What might I change this into?"

He lived all alone in a cave in the side of a mountain, and for years he never saw a living soul except his billy goat, because every time he heard footsteps coming, whether it was something real or something he'd created, he hid, sometimes by changing himself into thin air, sometimes by changing whatever *it* was into thin air, and sometimes by means more ingenious. The only thing he couldn't seem to change was, for some reason, dragons. And so he kept changing things to other things, insofar as possible, and refusing to look. It was just as well. It was by now the most curious country in the world, where the magic was out of control completely, and if the gnome had looked to see what creature was approaching him, real or otherwise, he might well have been frightened into his grave.

Sometimes what he would have seen would have been a dragon blowing smoke and fire and burning up the grass in front of him, making a road. Sometimes he would have seen two dragons, and sometimes three, or thirty, or three thousand. The whole country was crawling with dragons, as if somebody couldn't get enough of them, and all the people and all the birds and animals were terrified of them, including the billy goat, the gnome's only friend in the world. When the people of that country saw a dragon, they would shake so badly they'd set off small earthquakes. It was terrible. The only creature in the whole country who didn't shake (not counting the dragons) was the gnome. The reason was not so much that he was brave as that he was afraid of everything, whether or not he'd created it in the first place—rabbits, mice, chickens, even clock towers—but only mildly afraid, never having looked to see how bad it really was and knowing, moreover, that however ugly the thing might be, it wasn't as ugly as his own black-bearded, warty face, which was his main inspiration. He had, it should be added, an unusually strong constitution and couldn't be hurt too much by dragon fire. Besides, he knew the thing might not be there at all; more likely than not it was some magic he'd made up that had slipped his mind. So he merely shivered and hid, then went about his business.

The billy goat noticed how calm the gnome was, all things considered, when a dragon came near, and he thought about it, being very sly. He thought, "I ought to be able to make some *use* of this. It would make me my fortune." But he couldn't think exactly how to use it, though he thought and thought.

One day the king said, "That's enough! Those dragons are everywhere! I don't get a moment's peace! I decide to go riding and I find my horses are shaking so badly I can't sit on them. I decide to go dancing and I discover the band is too shaky to play anything but Greek. Death to the dragons!"

The people cheered, but when they asked the king how he meant to get rid of the dragons, he had no idea. The king said, "I'll give half my kingdom to whoever gets rid of the dragons."

The people all sighed. Who'd *want* such a mixed-up kingdom? But the billy goat, who was deeply, moaningly in love with the princess, scratched his chin and said, "How about the 'daughter's hand in marriage' part?"

"That too," said the king, not registering the fact that it was a billy goat who spoke. "Naturally. It goes without saying."

"Ah!" said the billy goat, and went home.

That night, when the gnome and the billy goat were eating supper, the billy goat said, "Well, well. So tonight's the night of the royal masked ball."

If there's one thing a gnome can't resist—even the shyest of gnomes—it's a royal masked ball. The elegance, the formality, the *art* of it all! And then—the best part—the gnome shows his horrible, horrible face at the center of all that grandeur and tinsel and sham, and the people go screaming and flying from the castle in hysterics, crying "Spoiler! Ruiner!" It makes a gnome so happy he feels downright faint.

"Ball?" said the gnome noncommitally.

The billy goat nodded.

"Hmm," said the gnome. He felt very nervous. Self-satisfied hermit that he was, he hated the thought of facing all those people, and yet—

"A ball, you say," he said.

"I know what you're thinking," the billy goat said. "Forget it. They're all in disguise, in hopes that if any gnome shows up the disguises will scare him to death. Their disguises will be so terrible you'll probably run from the guests before they even get a look at you." He chuckled.

"That's what *you* think," said the gnome.

"Well all right," said the billy goat, and shrugged. "I'll tell you where the ball is." And the billy goat directed his old friend to Dragons' Mountain. When the gnome was gone, the billy goat laughed and laughed.

The gnome found the dragons dancing in a ring in the center of the mountain, and thinking they were merely the king and his court in disguise, he walked right up to them, shy as he was, and looked them in the eye. To his great surprise they spit oily fire at him until his clothes were as black as soot. The gnome stamped his foot in anger and thought, "So!"

When the gnome got back to his own cave, the billy goat was sitting by the fire, and he too was black as soot, as if the same thing that had happened to the gnome had happened to everybody and it was certainly nothing special.

The gnome took a deep breath, not sure what was up, and all he could say was, "Billy goat, I expected more of you." And went to bed.

The billy goat stayed up late, chuckling and thinking.

The next night the billy goat said, "Well, well. So tonight's the night of the dooloo."

"Oh?" said the gnome.

If there's one thing a true gnome hates and detests, it's not knowing what somebody's talking about.

"It's tonight, is it?" the gnome said, not letting on that he didn't know about dooloos.

"Mmmm," said the billy goat indifferently.

"Where is it?" inquired the gnome.

As if wearily, the billy goat gave him directions, and although the directions sounded familiar, the gnome listened with all his ears, intending to go there and find out what the devil a dooloo was. He carefully followed the billy goat's directions, and sure enough, he ended up at Dragons' Mountain.

This time the dragons were waiting for him, and before he was halfway up the mountain, they rained down fire on him, and in a minute his clothes were black as soot and the hair of his beard was singed. He screamed with rage and pounded his fists and cried, "*So!*"

When he got home the billy goat was sitting by the fire looking calm and collected, though his beard was singed and he too was as black as soot.

"Billy goat," the gnome began.

But the billy goat said, "Well! So you've been wallawalled again!"

"Wallawalled?" said the gnome.

"Don't you know what 'wallawalled' means?" the billy goat asked innocently.

"Of course I do. Certainly!" said the gnome. Then, hastily, he went to bed.

Gnomes are no better than they might be, and neither are billy goats. Nevertheless, the gnome was not so stupid that he fell for the billy goat's trick on the third night.

The billy goat said, touching his beard with his right front hoof, "Well, well! So tonight's the night of the princess's pig roast!"

If there's one thing a gnome is totally indifferent to, it's a pig roast; and if there's another thing he's indifferent to, it's a princess. He felt, naturally, a strong temptation not to go to the princess's pig roast. But knowing that the billy goat was perhaps out to trick him—either into going or else into *not* going (he couldn't make out which)—he knew he must somehow do neither. He thought and thought.

"Where is it?" he said.

Indifferently, the billy goat gave him the same directions he'd given him last night and the night before—to Dragons' Mountain.

"So!" thought the gnome.

Then the gnome said, "How I wish I could go!" And then he said, "I know! I'll change you into me and me into you and then *you* can go."

"But I don't want to," the billy goat said.

"But you don't have to," said the gnome. "You'll be home all the time, because you'll be *me*, if you see what I mean."

The billy goat was no great logician, and it seemed to him he was trapped. At last, shaking like a leaf, the billy goat set out—changed into the outward appearance of the gnome—for Dragons' Mountain. "Old friend gnome," he said as he set out, "I expected more of you." Still, having no choice in the matter so far as he could see, he stepped gingerly on, and each rock he passed was darker and more ominous than the last. "Soon," he thought, "I will be at Dragons' Mountain. How ridiculous and sad!"

Meanwhile, back in the cave, the gnome chuckled at the trick he'd played on his old friend the billy goat. But little by little his chuckling stopped. The billy goat was, for better or worse, the only friend he had; and the gnome was not quite sure a billy goat superficially disguised as a gnome would have the tolerance for fire that a gnome had. "Suppose something should happen to my old friend!" he thought. Finally, leaping to his feet, he threw on his scarf and hurried toward the mountain.

Sure enough, when the gnome disguised as a billy goat got to Dragons' Mountain, there was his old friend the billy goat, disguised as a gnome, plodding sadly up the path toward the dragons' lair; and behind every tree, waiting until the billy goat disguised as a gnome should be surrounded, lurked a leering dragon.

The gnome disguised as a billy goat had no idea what to do, but he knew that in a moment those fires would start shooting and it would be goat roast. Before he stopped to think of a plan, the gnome disguised as a billy goat found himself rushing with his goat horns

55

lowered straight at the nearest of the dragons who, that moment, had turned his great spiny red and gold back. His goat horns threw the dragon high in the air, and the other dragons were so startled that they ran like sheep into a huddle. There they stood looking stupidly around to see what had caused all that terrible commotion. All at once they saw—really *saw*—the incredible ugly little gnome (really the billy goat), and it came to all of them at once that they'd never seen anything so ugly in their lives. They all began running in frantic circles, sometimes running into trees, sometimes running into boulders, sometimes running into each other. With each collision another dragon or two exploded, and the people watching from down in the valley thought for sure it was the end of the world. Soon all the dragons lay feet up, dead. With the last explosion, the mountain gave a shudder and collapsed on them and covered them completely.

The gnome turned himself back into himself and turned the billy goat back into the billy goat.

The gnome said, "Let this be a lesson to you, goat."

The billy goat apologized, but all the way home he smiled blissfully, thinking of the princess.

The next day, the billy goat went to see the king.

"Well," said the billy goat, "I got rid of those dragons for you. I'd like my reward."

"There's no such things as dragons," the king said, and tapped his large black pipe.

"What?" cried the billy goat, incredulous.

But no matter what the billy goat said, the king went on stubbornly acting as if he'd never heard of any dragons—changing all the rules with reckless abandon and insisting he'd never promised anyone half the kingdom or his daughter's hand in marriage. "That would be insane," he said.

The billy goat was furious and stomped until the palace—if it was a palace—shook. But the king merely smiled. "Let this be a lesson to you," he said, and the voice seemed familiar.

Now the billy goat was angrier than ever, realizing all at once that the king was really none other than the gnome, that the whole thing was fantasy and illusion! Then, abruptly, the billy goat stopped his stamping and dropped his mouth open, for he'd remembered that he himself was also the gnome. But if gnomes feel indifferent toward beautiful princesses, how could it be that—and now, horribly, it all came clear to him, and he burst out crying. He was also, obviously, the beautiful princess. "No question about it," said the gnome tragically, and struck his forehead with his hoof, "we've got to stop this fooling around and get back in touch."

John Gardner's first book for Children, *Dragon, Dragon,* was hailed by reviewers and readers of all ages. ". . . extraordinary tales laced with subtle wit and poignancy to bring out the message in the magic. It proves that a master storyteller's talents are applicable in any genre." (*Providence Sunday Journal*)

Gudgekin the Thistle Girl, which followed, proved that Gardner's imagination knew no bounds. And the four new stories in this third collection—another offbeat array of heroes and villains—confirm John Gardner's place as a teller of tales for readers and listeners of every age. His brilliant adult fiction includes *Nickle Mountain, The Sunlight Dialogues, The King's Indian,* and *Grendel.*

Michael Sporn was born and raised in New York City. After receiving his degree in Fine Arts, he began work in film animation. His credits include the feature-length film *Raggedy Ann and Andy* and *Everybody Rides the Carousel,* as well as numerous cartoons for *The Electric Company.* He also illustrated *Gudgekin the Thistle Girl,* which was his first book.